MAGICAL TALES FROM *Fairyland*

Meadow Fairies

Growing Wings

MAGICAL TALES FROM *Fairyland*

Meadow Fairies
Growing Wings

Ines Holmes

First published in the UK in 2022 by the Independent Publishing Network

Second edition containing a new cover and illustrations.

Author: Ines Holmes
Email: ines.holmes@icloud.com
Website: www.inesholmes.com
Please direct all enquiries to the author.

ISBN: 978-1-7398003-0-7

Written and illustrated by Ines Holmes

For my daughter
The real fairy in my life

CONTENTS

AN UNFORTUNATE EVENT

The sun rose gently over the late summer meadow. Most flowers were still in a deep slumber with their petals wrapped tightly around them. But in just a few hours, the meadow would be transformed from a sea of sparkling dew-drops to an ocean bursting with colour and vibrating with the buzzing of bees, the fluttering of butterflies and the crickety-crick of grasshoppers and other insects.

A ray of sun tickled Starflower's nose. She stretched her slender arms and legs, while shaking the morning dew off her wings. Her body was a translucent shade of pale pinks and blues, flowing through her like misty clouds. Starflower had spent the night sleeping on the leaf of a foxglove. Her mother, Meliantha, and father, Trillium, were sleeping on the leaf next to her.

Starflower and her parents are Meadow Fairies. These are small and delicate creatures, no bigger than a large butterfly. They have crystalline, shimmering bodies and wings, reflecting the colour of the sky and flowers around them – ever changing and always partly invisible, like a brilliant reflection of light on rippling water. They can also become invisible at will or change only the colour of their wings, to look like butterflies, which makes them incredibly difficult to spy.

"It's such a fine morning, Mother," said Starflower, "can I go and play with Sundrop? Please, Mother, can I?" Meadow Fairies of all ages love to play, but especially the younger ones.

"Of course you can," responded her mother, "but be back soon. We have to collect some nectar today. Summer is coming to an end and we need to make sure we gather enough nectar and honeydew for the colder months."

"I will, Mother. See you later," cried Starflower, who was already on her way to find her best friend Sundrop.

Meadow Fairy families live scattered across the entire meadow and change their sleeping places every night to avoid detection, but families that know each other well tend to stay fairly close together. Therefore, it didn't take Starflower very long to find Sundrop and her family.

Sundrop enjoyed watching the sunrise and warming-up her wings in the sun while having a sip of fresh morning dew, unlike her friend Starflower, who was always out and about as soon as the sun stretched her first pale rays of light across the meadow.

"Good morning, Starflower," called Sundrop. She

had already seen Starflower fluttering towards her. "You are up early…as usual," she added with a laugh that rang like crystal bells.

"Good morning!" Starflower smiled at her friend and her family. "Nothing like a refreshing flight through the morning mist! Let's go, Sundrop. I've seen some wonderful spider webs on the way here."

"Oh, that sounds amazing! Can I go, Mum, Dad?"

"Off you go," said her father, Vervain, "but be sure to be back in time to collect nectar, you two!"

"We will." The girls laughed in unison and fluttered away like dancing specks of light.

Now, you might wonder *What's so great about sticky spider webs?* You see, for a Meadow Fairy, a spider web full of delicate drops of morning dew is a most exciting thing. If the morning sun shines on it at just the right angle, it creates a wonderful spectre of smaller and bigger rainbows, which is not only beautiful to behold, but also an amazing playground. Meadow Fairies can slide down such rainbows just like human children can on slides in the park. The really big rainbows you can see across the sky can only be used by leprechauns, of course.

Starflower and Sundrop were in luck. Even from a distance they could see the kaleidoscopic dance of the rainbows shimmering on the spider webs. Down they slid first one rainbow, then another, and another, until they were out of breath, and laughing with delight.

"Oh, be careful!" Sundrop called out to Starflower, who nearly caught her wings in the web as she was rushing to the next rainbow. Fortunately, she managed to change direction just in time. Meadow Fairies might be immortal, but they can still get injured, especially on their fragile wings.

Soon, though, there were not enough dew-drops left, and the sun had risen higher in the sky. The little fairy girls had now taken on the colour of a hazy yellow, with bright clouds of blue, violet, red and pink rushing through them as they fluttered past the colourful meadow flowers, which were slowly opening their faces to the warm morning sun.

"Let's play Bouncy Petal," cried Sundrop, and they flew from one flower to the next, bouncing on each blossom, shaking off the last of the dew-drops and giggling all the way. A particularly large drop landed on a grasshopper underneath. He didn't look too pleased about this as he wiped the water off his wings.

"I'm so sorry," called Starflower over her shoulder, but she was already too far away for the grasshopper to hear. They finally sat down on a large purple blossom of a monkshood plant and looked across the meadow.

"I guess it will be autumn soon," said Sundrop. "Many flowers are losing their petals, and the grasses have turned more yellow than the bright, fresh green

they used to be."

"You're right. The nights are getting colder now as

well, and the days are so much shorter and don't warm up so much anymore. I guess we better get back and help our parents with the nectar."

Meadow Fairies don't store any food or drink over the spring and summer. There are plenty of flowers for everyone to drink from, and all of them taste differently. Some are really sweet and others have a sour or bitter aftertaste, and some even sting a little bit on the tongue. The fairies also drink the fresh morning dew from the petals and leaves. For a special treat, they ask the bees for some meadow honey or they make spicy mead from the tiny seeds of meadow grasses. Towards the end of summer, however, Meadow Fairies start to store nectar for the cooler months, when the flowers have lost their blossoms and the meadow is slowly dying, just to return with renewed strength and colour the next year. During this time, they go into hibernation until spring, as they don't care for the cold and wet weather. As soon as the last meadow flowers have died off, they join the Stone Fairies, who live in dry stone walls alongside fields and forests. They spend a few weeks in each other's company, exchanging stories and wisdom from the elders, and celebrating their short union, until November Eve, when the Meadow Fairies withdraw to the most concealed and protected holes in the wall to hibernate. The Stone Fairies watch over them and enjoy the nectar and honeydew the Meadow

Fairies have brought with them, always keeping some in spare for the Meadow Fairies to drink when they wake up again. It gives them strength for their journey back to their meadows.

Starflower and Sundrop found their parents, who were already busy collecting nectar from the flowers that were still in bloom.

"There you are!" called Meliantha. "We thought you had forgotten all about your chores today."

There was a twinkling in her eyes and a smile on her lips. She had never been able to seriously be cross with her daughter. Who didn't enjoy a bit of fun and play?

"We have already filled these corncockle blossoms," said Sundrop's mother, Merrybell, pointing at a number of funnel-shaped blossoms, neatly tied up with blades of meadow grass. "Can you take them to the burrow, please? But do be careful not to drop them!"

"Don't worry, Mother, we will be careful," said Sundrop, and both girls picked up a blossom and fluttered off to the burrow.

Meadow Fairies find an empty rabbit burrow or tunnel left behind by moles, rats or mice to gather together their food for the winter.

The closer the fairy girls got to the burrow, the busier the meadow got. Fairies fluttered towards it from all directions of the meadow, all now shimmering brightly in the midday sun. Everyone was so busy, Starflower and Sundrop had to wait a good while just to drop their blossoms off. Once they had entered the burrow, they were awestruck by the amount of nectar-filled blossoms around them.

"Look!" exclaimed Starflower. "The blossoms are stacked right up to the ceiling. And it smells so good… yummy! It's making me really hungry. Let's go and find some nectar for ourselves."

"But we have to make at least two more trips just to drop off the blossoms our parents have already filled. We can't just let them lie there."

"Alright, alright. Let's go then, but after that we eat and play Seek the Fairy."

"Alright," giggled Sundrop.

But there were so many blossoms to take to the burrow now that the girls didn't have any time to play that day, nor the next one, or the day after that. The days were quickly getting shorter, colder and windier, and the fairies were all busy with the final preparations before they would join the Stone Fairies.

This is no fun at all, thought Starflower to herself one morning. *I don't want to spend the last days of summer carrying nectar to the burrow. Surely it won't hurt if I go out to play for a bit? Just a couple of hours?*

The morning was cool, and dark clouds were massing in the sky. It would be raining soon, but that didn't stop Starflower. Off she fluttered across the meadow looking for a little adventure.

I'll go and find Sundrop first, she thought. *I'm sure she'd love to come as well.*

She soon found Sundrop busy at work helping her parents. Sundrop was just about to set off with another petal filled with delicious nectar. Starflower followed her at a distance until they were out of her parent's sight, then quickly caught up with her.

"Hallo, Sundrop! Let's have a race."

"Huh? Oh, it's you!" said Sundrop. "Shouldn't you be helping your parents?"

"Yes, I know, but the last few days have been so dull, and this will probably be our last chance before we go into hibernation."

"I know, Starflower, but I really have to bring this blossom to the burrow," said Sundrop, although she was as keen as Starflower to have a bit of fun.

"You can hide it here and we'll take it to the burrow together later. We'll only be gone for a little while. Please, Sundrop," pleaded Starflower.

"Alright then, but only for a little bit."

They hid the blossom and fluttered away. Both fairy girls loved to race across the meadow, brushing past the flowers and grasses that were now bent down by the wind. Soon, it also started to rain, but still they flew faster and faster until…

“Oh, help!”

A strong gush of wind had picked Sundrop up and blown her sideways into the hooked burs of a burdock plant! Her wings got pinned to the plant as the spiky burs tore into them.

“Sundrop!” gasped Starflower. She turned around and flew back to help her friend.

“Don’t come too close, Starflower, or the same

might happen to you."

"Can you free your wings?"

Sundrop wriggled around trying to release her wings from the hooks, but that only made it worse.

"I'm stuck! You have to get help, Starflower."

"This is all my fault. I should never have convinced you to come with me!" cried Starflower.

"It was my own choice, but you have to get my parents. Be quick! Every gush of wind is pushing the burs deeper into my wings."

"I'll be as quick as I can!" Starflower rushed back to get help, while poor Sundrop was pinned to the burs swaying in the wind. Luckily, fairies don't experience pain the same way as humans do, otherwise this would have been a very excruciating experience for little Sundrop.

In the meantime, both their parents were getting uneasy. They had suspected that their daughters had snuck off to enjoy a few moments of freedom before winter, but the children had been gone a while now, and it was not like them to neglect their duties for so long.

"I'm worried something might have happened to our dear child," Meliantha said to Trillium.

"You worry too much, Meliantha. Starflower is a bright little fairy, she can look after herself."

"I know, but still. I'd rather we went looking for her. Let's find Merrybell and Vervain. Maybe she's flown over there to play with Sundrop."

They soon found them collecting nectar from some columbines nearby.

"Hello, Merrybell. Have you seen Starflower?"

"No, I'm afraid I haven't," said Merrybell. "But Sundrop also hasn't returned from her trip to the burrow yet. They have probably gone to play a bit. Though it has been a while now, I have to say, and the weather is turning nasty."

"We should go looking for them. I'm worried something might have happened," said Meliantha.

"But where shall we start?" asked Trillium. "The meadow is huge, and what if they come back in the meantime?"

Just as Meliantha was about to respond, she saw her daughter rushing towards them in great haste. She was completely out of breath as she landed on the leaf next to her mother.

"Where is Sundrop?" cried Merrybell.

"Wind…hooks…burs…can't…free herself," panted Starflower.

"Catch your breath, child, and then tell us what happened," said Meliantha, trying to soothe her daughter.

Collecting herself, Starflower explained what had

happened a little more slowly.

"I'm so sorry," she sobbed.

"Come, Starflower, can you show us the way? We have to free Sundrop as soon as we can," said Vervain.

They all set off together. The weather was getting worse. Black clouds were coming in and the wind whistled across the meadow.

And how had poor Sundrop fared during all this time? She had been desperately trying to free herself, but only damaged her wings even more. The strong wind kept pressing her into the hooks of the bur. She was now trying to stay as still as possible, hoping that Starflower would soon return with her parents, but it was getting dark quickly. Suddenly, she saw a group of sparkling lights in the last light of the day, coming straight towards her.

"I'm over here!" Sundrop shouted as loudly as she could. They had found her.

"Oh my dear, poor child. We'll get you out of there."

"We can't get too close, otherwise we'll get blown into the burs as well," said Vervain. "We have to find a flower stem or stick that we can use to free Sundrop's wings."

He and Trillium returned in just a few minutes. In the meantime, Meliantha had taken a better look at the damage to Sundrop's wings, while Merrybell tried to comfort her daughter.

"I'm afraid she won't be able to fly once her wings are free, they are too badly injured," said Meliantha.

"We will have to catch her when she falls, then," Vervain responded. "Trillium and I will free up her wings with the flower stems and you two catch her," said Vervain. They cautiously set to work while Merrybell and Meliantha hovered underneath Sundrop, cautious not to be blown into the burs themselves.

"Not long now, my darling. Don't worry, we will catch you," said Merrybell.

It was very precarious work, but eventually they succeeded in levering Sundrop's wings from the hooks, and she dropped safely into the arms of her mother and Meliantha, who then flew her off to a plant nearby. Merrybell hugged her daughter tightly and Vervain joined the embrace.

Starflower was riddled with guilt.

"She'll be okay," she heard her mother's whisper in her ear, who had landed beside her, giving her hand a squeeze.

"We have to find a safe place to spend the night. It's too dangerous to carry Sundrop in this wind, and it's too dark to see now anyway," said Trillium after a few minutes.

They all passed the night together on the leaves of a

coneflower without any further incidents. Luckily, the next morning dawned brightly and they sat down together over a rich breakfast of sweet nectar that soon revived their energy and spirit. But what was there to be done about Sundrop's torn wings? Meadow Fairies have great self-healing powers, but her wings were too damaged even for that.

"You should consult the queen," said Meliantha. "She'll know what to do."

"Then we better summon her quickly," said Merrybell.

THE QUEEN OF THE MEADOW FAIRIES

The Queen of the Meadow Fairies is the greatest healer of their folk. She knows magical spells and can brew strong potions that no other Meadow Fairy knows of. She is the bearer of the most precious gem stone of the Meadow Fairies. It is shaped like a raindrop, and although it looks crystal clear, it appears to carry the bluest skies, the brightest sunlight and the most vibrant colours of meadow flowers within it. Like the rest of the Meadow Fairies, their queen, Orchidalia, doesn't have a fixed abode, but travels from meadow to meadow across the entire fairy realm. There, she will give advice and extend her healing powers where they are needed, but mainly she will listen to tales and news from the fairies, and share tales with them from other Meadow Fairies she has come across. She has immense knowledge of tales and adventures, which is why the other fairies are always eagerly awaiting her next visit.

It doesn't often happen that the queen has to be consulted in urgent matters. Meadow Fairies are a peaceful folk and can generally take good care of themselves. But every now and then, her healing powers and advice are urgently needed, and in those cases it is possible to summon the queen. Every Meadow Fairy wears their personal crystal around their neck, which they receive from their parents when they are born, and which also determines the dominant hue in their bodies. It doesn't just protect them against evil spirits, but is also their connection to the queen. If fairies join their crystals, the summoning spell is enhanced significantly, which gives the queen additional speed. And this is what Sundrop and her family and friends now did. All six of them sat down together on a big leaf and put their crystals in the middle around Sundrop's crystal. As they joined their hands, they started to sing in their beautiful crystal glass voices:

> "Queen of the Meadows, hear our plea,
> A fairy is in need of help from thee.
> Across the meadows South and North,
> Please come to us, we call you forth."

"What happens now?" asked Sundrop. She was still quite shaken by the recent events and very worried about her wings, but she was also sure the queen would be able to help her.

"Now, we wait," said her mother. "We don't know where the queen is at the moment. The summoning charm will give her speed, but it may still take a few days for her to get here."

And so they waited. As Sundrop was unable to fly, she was brought to a safe place every day where she would have a good view over the meadow, and could keep an eye out for the queen's arrival. Starflower worked twice as hard to make up for Sundrop not being able to help with the nectar collecting now. She had gone very quiet since Sundrop's accident. She went to see her every day, but although Sundrop never blamed her for anything, she still felt quite uncomfortable in her presence now. Her mother tried to console her, reassuring her that everything would be okay again, but that didn't really help.

After three days, they finally saw the queen approaching. Well, it was not so much the queen they saw. Instead, the entire meadow was suddenly in such a stir. Everything in the meadow – plants, insects and fairies – was greatly excited all of a sudden, humming and vibrating as if electrically charged. The queen had arrived!

Starflower and the others rushed back to where Sundrop was hidden for the day, because that's where the queen would be drawn towards. She was already there when Starflower arrived, closely followed by both their parents. The fairy girls were in utter awe of the queen. They had never seen her so close. Queen

Orchidalia was bigger than the other Meadow Fairies and of extraordinary beauty. She didn't reflect the colours around her in her crystalline body as the other Meadow Fairies did, but seemed to emit light and colour herself. Simply being in the queen's presence made them feel light-hearted and hopeful. All worries and guilt were forgotten and replaced by love and happiness.

"My dear Sundrop," began the queen.

"How do you know my name?" Sundrop asked in surprise.

"I know the names of all Meadow Fairies. But now tell me, what has happened to your wings?"

The events were quickly retold.

The queen took Sundrop by the hands and smiled at her gently. "Poor little Sundrop. You should have been more careful flying out in that weather. We Meadow Fairies have to take good care of our wings. I'm afraid that healing your wings exceeds even my healing powers. But fret not, there is a different way, although it is dangerous, and time is of the essence."

"What other way, dearest queen?" enquired Merrybell. "We'll do anything for our daughter."

"Instead of healing her wings, Sundrop will have to grow new wings," answered the queen.

"New wings? I didn't even know we could do that!" said Sundrop.

"Well, it doesn't happen very often that a fairy injures her wings beyond repair," said the queen with a wink, "and it requires a very difficult ritual that has to be performed on November Eve just before we go into hibernation, so your wings can regrow while you are asleep." Orchidalia explained further, "but that is not all. I require a special elixir for this ritual, one only our cousins, the Highland Fairies, know how to make. Without it, the ritual won't work. Someone will have to find King Teague, ask him to prepare the elixir and return with it to the Stone Fairies in time for November Eve. I won't be able to go myself, as I will have to make other preparations for the ritual."

There was a moment's silence. Even with the queen's beautiful aura of light, they felt the direness of the situation. Fly all the way to the Highland Fairies, find the king and return before November Eve? They had only five weeks, so it was indeed a most time sensitive, let alone dangerous, mission.

"I'll go," exclaimed Vervain. "I'm her father, of course I'll be the one to go."

"But Vervain, we will need you here to help with the transport of the blossoms to the Stone Fairies," Trillium said.

The grown-up fairies started to discuss the matter of who should be the one to go on this perilous journey, when Starflower got up and said: "I'll go!"

The adults stared at her for a moment, then her mother said: "Oh no, you won't. It is much too dangerous."

"But you are all needed here, and I know I can do it."

Before anyone could argue with Starflower, the

queen took her aside. “My dear Starflower, I believe you want to do this because you feel responsible for Sundrop’s situation and want to make amends. However, it would be quite foolish to endanger yourself like this to ease your conscience. It is a perilous journey that lies ahead, and should not be taken lightly.”

“I understand, Queen Orchidalia. I do indeed feel responsible for what has happened to Sundrop, but she’s my best friend in the world and I know I can do it. Please, I do understand the danger.”

The queen looked gravely at Starflower and considered for a while. Then her gaze softened again and she put her hand gently on her shoulder.

“You shall have my blessing. I’ll cast a protective spell on you and give you a special tonic that will give you strength. I shall return at first light tomorrow morning, then you must set off.”

With that, the queen fluttered away.

The others had watched them and didn’t need any further explanation. It was quite clear that Starflower had received the queen’s permission to go, and none of them questioned the wisdom of the queen’s decision.

Queen Orchidalia returned at first light the next morning as promised. She first spoke to both parents to reassure them that their girls would be alright. Then, she gave Starflower instructions on how to find her way to the Highland Fairies and where to find King

Teague. Initially, she would be able to find shelter with other Meadow Fairies along the way, but the further North she travelled, the longer the distances between the Meadow Fairy folks would be. There were also a great many lakes to fly around, and heathlands and moors to cross, which are full of Goblins and evil spirits. The weather would also be getting worse as the weeks progressed towards November Eve.

Then she gave Starflower the tonic and cast the protective spell over her. Lastly, she turned to Sundrop:

"Be patient, Sundrop, you will have wings again! I must go and start my own preparations now. I wish all of you a safe journey and shall see you again on November Eve."

As the queen fluttered away, the two fairy families gathered closely together to say their goodbyes to Starflower. They wouldn't be able to help her now and could only await her safe return with the much-needed elixir. Starflower and Sundrop hugged tightly, with tears rolling down their cheeks.

"Do be careful, I beg you, Starflower," said Sundrop.

"Don't worry, I will return in time, with the elixir."

Before she finally set off, Meliantha took her daughter aside. "You have taken a great burden upon yourself, my child. I know I can't talk you out of it, but please, do be careful. There are more dangers out there than you are aware off. The queen's charm will protect you, but don't be reckless. Come back safe."

THE JOURNEY BEGINS

Starflower felt sad and scared to leave the safety of the meadow and her family behind her, but she was also determined to bring back the elixir from the Highland Fairies. Armed with the protective charm and strengthening tonic, she soon left the familiar borders of her home meadow behind her. She passed two other fairy meadows on her first day, but didn't stop to spend the night there as there was still enough daylight left to go on. But when night fell, there was no other meadow in sight, so poor Starflower had to spend the first night all on her own. She found a large pond and settled on a cane reed for the night. She spent a very restless night there. She had heard about Asrai living in waters like this. The Asrai are water nymphs. Some say they are gentle creatures, but unsocial, others say they are vengeful when crossed. Starflower hoped this pond wasn't occupied, because, gentle or not, she didn't much like the idea of making the acquaintance of an Asrai in the middle of the night.

The wind whistled eerily through the reeds, but

finally, Starflower managed to fall asleep. The night passed without any surprises from an Asrai or other creature, but Starflower had a rude awaking as two ducks squeezed their way through the reeds and nearly shook her off the cane. She found some nectar for her breakfast, then set off again.

The weather was pleasant, and she made good progress. A few hours later she sat down on a shrub to rest for a while.

I hope I'll be able to spend the night with other Meadow Fairies tonight, she thought. *It was not pleasant on that reed!*

Soon she was off again, and this time she was in luck. Just as it was beginning to get dark, she approached a meadow that was humming with the fluttering of fairy wings.

"Hello," she called to the first fairy she saw.

"Oh, hello," said the other fairy, much surprised. "I don't think I have seen you in this meadow before."

"My name is Starflower, and my meadow is two day's journey to the South."

"My name is Celandine. What brings you to our meadow? It's very unusual behaviour for a Meadow Fairy to leave their own meadow – apart from our queen, of course."

"It is our queen who has sent me this way. I am on my way to the King of the Highland Fairies to ask him for an elixir. I was hoping to find shelter in this meadow tonight."

"You shall be most welcome, Starflower. I will inform the others. It is so exciting to have a visitor from another meadow."

"Thank you, Celandine. That is very kind of you."

And so Starflower spent the night among newfound friends. She had to tell them the entire story about the reason for her journey to the Highland Fairies, of course, and everyone gasped as they heard that poor Sundrop would have to regrow her wings. They, in return, shared some of their stories with her, and so it was quite late when Starflower finally went to sleep. Early the next morning she said goodbye to Celandine and a few of the others and set off again.

The next few days and nights passed without any major incidents. Starflower was lucky enough to spent two more nights with other Meadow Fairies, and was made just as welcome as she had been by Celandine.

After a week of travelling, Starflower was beginning to get weary. She also wasn't quite sure how much further she'd have to go before she'd reach the Highlands. She hadn't even reached the big lakes yet.

Suddenly, she saw something glisten in the distance, like a shimmering silver ribbon along the horizon. She had reached the first lake! As dusk would be approaching soon, she resolved to rest in a shrub near the lake

and to decide which route to take in the morning light.

As it was getting dark, Starflower heard something rustling in the leaves at the bottom of the shrub she had chosen as her night shelter.

What is this noise? she wondered. *I've never heard anything like it.* Very carefully and as quietly as she could, Starflower fluttered a little lower to see where the noise was coming from. But before she could even call out, something long and sticky came shooting towards her through the dying leaves. Just as it was about to touch her, she was blinded by bright light, like a flash, directly in front of her eyes. She screamed and flew back up to the highest branches.

"What was that?" she panted, out of breath, her little heart pounding. The creature must have been equally frightened by the sudden light and had disappeared into the night.

After a few minutes, Starflower managed to compose herself again and thought about what had just occurred. *The light*, she thought, *that will have been the queen's protective spell. That must have been the horrible tongue of a toad trying to eat me, mistaking me for a butterfly. Without the spell, he would have succeeded!*

Never before had Starflower felt so vulnerable and alone, and she began to cry. But then she remembered the queen's strengthening tonic. With shaking hands, she took a sip and felt hope, warmth and confidence flowing through her body. It was as if her mother was there with her, giving her a loving embrace. Starflower curled up on a leaf, still feeling the warmth and comfort of her mother's arms, like a warm blanket, and fell asleep.

She woke up well-rested and refreshed the next morning and ventured closer to the lake. It was so large she couldn't even see the other side, no matter how high she flew up into the air!

"What am I to do now?" she asked aloud. "I might lose too much time if I fly around it, but what if I can't reach the other side before I get too tired to cross it? I will drown in its waters."

She sat in the grass along the shoreline, pondering what to do.

"It's no use," she said to herself. "I have to continue one way or another. I will take another large swallow of the tonic the queen has given me and try my luck straight across."

Starflower felt the tonic flow through her body and fill her with titillating energy and confidence. She set off across the lake immediately.

Even with the magic tonic, it was very hard work. The further she flew away from the shoreline the windier it got, and Starflower was blown off her path more than once, but she kept going. At one point, she was entirely surrounded by water, with no land in sight whatsoever. But then, after many exhausting hours, and just before it was starting to get dark again, she saw the other side. She took another sip from the tonic, and with the destination in sight, she managed to speed up and land safely in the grass on the other side of the lake. Poor Starflower was too exhausted to even find a safer place to spend the night, and fell into a deep sleep.

When she woke up the next morning, she found herself surrounded by a flock of sheep that had come out to drink water from the lake. She was very lucky she hadn't been trampled on or eaten by accident. She immediately rose into the air, but found that her wings were hurting a great deal after the extraordinary efforts of the day before and landed on the back of a sheep.

"Ow," she cried. "I must have pulled the muscles in my wings yesterday. Oh, what am I to do now?"

Just then, she saw a group of young Meadow Fairies, singing and laughing, as they fluttered towards the lake.

"Hallo," called Starflower, "please, will you come and help me?"

The fairies looked around and saw Starflower standing on the back of the sheep waving her arms. They flew to her in great excitement. Chatting all at once, they bombarded Starflower with a barrage of questions.

"Where do you come from?" asked one.

"What are you doing here?" asked another.

"What's your name?" asked the third.

"Please, my dear fairies, I'll tell you everything you want to know, but first I need your help. My wings are hurting badly from crossing this lake yesterday."

"You flew across the lake?" they asked, astonished.

"Yes, I'm on my way to the Kind of the Highland Fairies. I need to speak to him urgently."

"It's still a long way to where the Highland King lives," said one of the girls who went by the name of Cicely. "You better come with us and speak to Gentian. He's the wisest fairy in our meadow and will know what to do."

"But I can't fly. My wings are hurting too much," replied Starflower.

"Oh, I know," said another fairy girl, called May-apple. "We'll find a big leaf for Starflower to sit on and carry her back to the meadow."

"That's a great idea," cheered the others.

They carried Starflower on the leaf of a wild rose bush, chatting and giggling all the way. When Star-flower told them about the purpose of her journey, they nearly dropped her in their amazement. They finally reached the meadow and found Gentian busy collect-ing nectar. Just as in Starflower's own meadow, these fairies were preparing for winter.

"You have taken on a very big responsibility," said Gentian, when Starflower had finished telling her story. "And I'm afraid you'll need to rest here a while before you can continue. You have strained your wings immensely and they need to rest to let them heal again," he continued. "You also have three more big lakes like this to cross before you reach the moors."

"But I don't have much time left to find King Teague, and I don't even really know yet where I can find him," cried Starflower in despair.

"There may be another way to pass the lakes more quickly," said Gentian.

"What other way?" asked Starflower.

"I'll have to make some enquiries first," said Gentian. "Eat and rest, I'll be back as soon as I can."

Starflower tried to relax, but was quite uneasy. Her thoughts were continuously going back to Sundrop and her family.

Were they alright? Were they already on their way to the Stone Fairies? Where had Gentian gone, and what was that other way he talked about?

Starflower wasn't to find out until the next morning, and spent a very restless night feeling anxious and worried.

She eventually fell asleep, and woke with a start the next morning. Starflower paced uneasily on her leaf, her wings still hurting too much to fly, when Cicely, Mayapple and the other fairy girls from the day before arrived with some nectar and fresh morning dew.

"Has Gentian returned?" Starflower asked, before taking a large gulp of the nectar. It tasted different to the nectar of her home meadow, somehow richer and spicier.

"No, I'm afraid he hasn't," replied Cicely.

"I wonder where he's gone," said Mayapple. "He's been away all night."

They tried their best to distract Starflower, but it was quite obvious that she wasn't really listening. Around midday, Gentian finally returned. He looked exhausted and it was apparent that he hadn't slept.

"I've been to speak to the Asrai," Gentian said in response to their questioning looks. The fairy girls gasped. Starflower was the first to speak.

"I've heard about the Asrai, but wasn't sure if they were real or just a myth. Are they not supposed to be vicious?"

"Oh, they exist alright," said Gentian. "They are not the most welcoming or sociable creatures to be around, but they are not as bad as their reputation. They are actually quite helpful and gentle – when you know their customs and how to talk to them, that is."

"Do you mean to say that the Asrai will be able to help me?" Starflower asked amazed. "How?"

"Well, over many, many years, the Asrai have built tunnels deep underwater that connect the big lakes. They allow them to move freely around the four biggest lakes instead of being stuck in only one."

"But how is that going to help me?" asked Starflower.

"The Asrai will create a transport bubble, which will allow one of them to take you through the tunnels right to the other side of the lakes within just a few hours. The Asrai are fast swimmers."

"And they would do that for me?" Starflower asked, surprised.

"Well, yes," replied Gentian. "As I said, they are really quite helpful when you know how to talk to them. But I will have to fill you in on some of their formalities before you leave, and you have to be aware that you will spend several hours in absolute darkness! First, though, I need to rest, and so should you: you'll set off tonight."

With that, Gentian fluttered away to rest, leaving the other fairies gazing after him, open-mouthed. It took a few minutes before any of them could say a word.

"Are you really going to do this, Starflower?" asked

Cicely.

"What choice do I have? I've lost two days already and still have the moors to cross. I have to trust that the protective spell Queen Orchidalia has cast on me will protect me through this as well."

The girls were quiet for a long time. Later in the afternoon, Gentian returned to explain to Starflower what she'd have to do and how to behave with the Asrai so as not to anger them. By the end of it, her head was spinning with all the instructions. She was afraid she wouldn't remember all of them, but she was also keen to continue her journey. Time was pressing.

CROSSING THE LAKES

As soon as the moon had risen, Starflower and Gentian flew back to the lake where they were awaited by two Asrai. One appeared to be a mature female, while the other one looked much younger. The fairies landed on the shore and Gentian saluted the Asrai in their own language. After the formalities had been exchanged, the older of the two Asrai addressed Starflower directly. She was about 3 feet tall and had long seaweed-like hair that stuck to her head, which was the only part of her body that was out of the water. The Asrai have incredibly sensitive skin, which is why they had to meet in the light of the moon. Her skin was a pale shade of green, her hands were webbed and she had a fishtail instead of legs. Gills on both sides of their neck allow the Asrai to breath underwater, but they can also breath air for short periods of time.

Her eyes were big and iridescent, and looked like they were glowing in the moonlight. Even though her teeth were sharp and pointed, her face was beautiful and friendly-looking. She looked eerie but not threatening.

"I am Eiddwen, and this is my daughter Alwen," she said, sounding hoarse, and gasping slightly for air. "Alwen will take you through our tunnels to the other side of the lakes."

Alwen looked very much like her mother, but was nearly a foot smaller. She had the same, eerily glowing eyes as her mother, but there was also a sparkle that told of a love for fun and adventure.

Starflower looked at them in amazement. Never would she have imagined that she would meet Asrai on her journey, let alone travel with them underwater. She eventually found her voice again and thanked Eiddwen and Alwen for their great kindness. She had taken an immediate liking to Alwen.

"You should set off now," said Gentian. "Alwen will form a transport bubble, but you'll have to enter it underwater. Fold your wings as tightly as you can and step on Alwen's hand. You'll have to hold your breath for a few seconds until you can step into the bubble. Good luck, and may the rest of your journey be safe."

Starflower was getting very nervous now. She thanked Gentian for his immeasurable help, folded her wings tightly to her body and stepped onto Alwen's palm, which felt wet and cold. She felt Alwen's hand gently close around her so she wouldn't float away. The cold water rose higher and higher around her, and just before it reached her chest, she took a deep breath and disappeared under the surface of the lake.

Her heart racing, she opened her eyes and found herself directly in front of the bubble. Alwen gently pushed her in and Starflower felt the bubble closing behind her. It took a moment before she dared to breath, but when she did, perfectly fresh air filled her lungs, although it had a strong smell of seaweed and fish. Before Starflower realised what was happing, Alwen had flicked herself around and dived into the dark depths of the lake.

With just the moonlight to light up the night, they were soon surrounded by the absolute darkness of the lake. Every now and then, Starflower saw an even darker shadow zoom past. "Probably a fish," she tried to calm herself. She found this situation very unnerving.

"Don't worry, I will keep you safe," Alwen suddenly said. She hadn't spoken a single word so far. Unlike her mother's, Alwen's voice was soft, like gentle waves rolling to shore.

"Our voices sound much gentler underwater," she continued, intuiting Starflower's thoughts.

"I— I didn't realise we would be able to speak on the journey," said Starflower. She looked at Alwen and saw the dim glow of her eyes, slightly illuminating their surroundings.

"It will take us all night to cross the three lakes.

Nothing much happens here. It is so nice to finally have some company. Tell me, what is it like on the surface? I only ever get to see the shoreline in the light of the moon."

Starflower told her about the meadow, and her best friend Sundrop. She told her about the accident and about the purpose of her journey. In return, Alwen told her about her life in the lakes. All the while, Alwen swam with what felt to Starflower like immense speed through the lakes and tunnels.

"How do you even know where you're going in this darkness?" asked Starflower.

"I can actually see very well," said Alwen. "Our eyes are very well adapted to these low levels of light. I can also kind of feel my surroundings. It's difficult to explain. I just know."

Talking like this, the hours passed very quickly and dawn was soon upon them.

"We're nearly there now, but we must hurry. I won't be able to take you to the surface if the sun is up."

Very slowly, Starflower became able to distinguish shapes around her. She looked up and saw the surface of the water several feet above her.

"Oh no," said Alwen. "It is later than I thought. It will be too dangerous for me to take you all the way up to the surface."

"What shall we do?"

"I will push the bubble towards the surface. It will pop as soon as it breaks the surface, so you'll have to be quick to fly out of it before the water closes over you."

"How can I ever thank you?"

"It was so nice to have company. And if you need a ride back, just call my name underwater and I'll be there by nighttime."

"But I can't speak underwater!" responded Starflower.

"Don't worry, I'll still hear you."

Then Alwen gently pushed the bubble upwards. They waved at each other. Just before the bubble touched the surface, Starflower spread her wings and burst through to the fresh morning air. She found herself about 50 feet from the shore. She was very glad to be above the water again, and even happier to have found a new friend. Still exhilarated by the experience, she immediately set off northward, towards the moors.

THE MOORS

The landscape soon changed. It became rockier, hillier and more barren. After just a few hours of flying, Starflower saw vast fields of heather spread out in front of her. A cold wind blew, taking with it the last bit of excitement Starflower had felt after a night of swimming through the depth of the lakes with Alwen. She sat down on a rock overlooking the landscape before her and tried to remember what Queen Orchidalia had told her:

"The heathland and moors are the last frontier before you reach the realm of King Teague, and it is the most dangerous land for fairies to cross. It is inhabited by Goblins and evil spirits who live in the crags and bogs, trying to lead other creatures astray with eerie howls and confusing lights.

Travel only by daylight, and fly as high as the wind allows you, for it is a cold harsh wind that will expect you there. Find a safe resting place for the night well before it gets dark, and never attempt to cross a bog or moor when the light is already fading. You can drink the nectar of the heather, but it's much spicier and more bitter than you're used to.

Find a crack in a rock to spend the night. And never, ever spend a night on an open moor!"

So far, Starflower had been met by hospitality and friendliness on her journey, but Queen Orchidalia's warnings didn't leave much hope for finding these qualities here.

She drank some heather nectar, which was indeed very bitter despite the flower's sweet scent. After a brief rest, she continued her journey, flying as high as possible without being blown off her course by the wind. Every now and then she saw something moving quickly among the heather, but she couldn't tell if it was an animal or something else. It seemed to be following her, so Starflower didn't dare to land for a long time. Eventually, daylight was slowly fading and she was forced to find a safe resting place for the night. Before her was a group of rugged, craggy rocks, which could provide her with the necessary protection and disguise. She indeed found a crack that was just big enough for her to crawl into. There she would be sheltered from the weather and hopefully also from any ill-meaning creatures.

Before crawling in, she flew a bit lower to pick a couple of heather blossoms to drink from later, when she suddenly heard a rushing through the bushes, and a grunting noise coming towards her. Scared, she immediately turned invisible, retreating quickly to the crack in the rock and crawling in. It was at first difficult to hear any sounds over the beating of her heart. But when nothing further happened, Starflower started to relax a bit again, though she didn't dare venture out again that evening.

All night, Starflower was kept awake by the howling of the wind and strange grunting noises that were sometimes closer and sometimes further away, like animals on the hunt. She was very glad when the sun finally rose again. She waited until it was high up in the sky before leaving the safety of the crack. By now, she was very hungry indeed. She didn't want to drink any more of the queen's tonic unless absolutely necessary. Carefully scanning her surroundings, she picked some heather blossoms and took them to one of the larger boulders to drink.

Taking a closer look at the landscape, she realised that a large bog lay before her. The days were quickly getting shorter now, and she couldn't see the other side from where she was, so she decided to quickly set off again.

She couldn't see anything unusual at first, and focussed on the horizon, searching for the end of the bog. But then she saw something moving underneath her again, and this time she could get a better glimpse. A greyish creature about the size of a rat, with a large head, claw-like hands and feet, which it used to run like a dog. It had big, bat-like ears and horrible eyes, and it was clearly following her path.

This must be a Goblin, thought Starflower. *I'm sure it was him yesterday as well, sniffing all around my hiding place. I do hope the queen's spell will protect me against him, too. How will I ever get rid of him?*

As the day went on, Starflower thought she'd lost him once or twice, but then she would see him again not far behind.

I can't even stop to rest because of him, and now it's getting dark and I still can't see the end of the bog. The queen said not to spend the night in a bog, so I have to go on. I should probably take a sip of the tonic, I'm getting very tired.

Invigorated by the tonic, Starflower sped up in an attempt to outfly the Goblin. It was getting dark now and she could see strange lights shimmering underneath her. Among them was a pair of orange-yellow glowing eyes still following her trail. Starflower

realised with despair that the first set off eyes had now been joined by a second.

"I can't just keep flying until I reach the Highlands! Do those creatures never rest?" she exclaimed.

Starflower was now terrified. She could hardly make out what was underneath her. Meadow Fairies can't see very well in the dark, while the Goblin's eyesight improves at night. Losing the fight against her exhaustion, Starflower slowly descended. Suddenly, she was attacked by the two Goblins, who had jumped at her out of nowhere from both sides. Starflower screamed and saw the blindingly bright light again. It was much more powerful this time than with the toad. Both Goblins bounced off her and were catapulted several feet away from her. Grunting and screeching, they lay on the soggy ground. Illuminated by the intense bright light, Starflower saw their frog-like mouths with sharp pointy teeth. Their noses were flat and broad, with slits for nostrils. Their faces were frightful and contorted. As soon as Starflower was able, she rushed onwards in the dark. She was still in a panic and didn't watch where she was flying. All she could think was, *Away, away, away!*

She didn't know how she got there, but she had finally reached the other side of the bog. Now, a steep rocky hill lay before her. She could make out a huge dark shape in front of her. As she got closer, she found strange round caves hewn into the surface of the rock. They were just big enough for Starflower, and so she crawled into the highest one she could find and passed out with exhaustion. She was too tired even to worry about who or what may have made these holes.

When Starflower woke up, a pale sun was already high up in the sky. She felt confused and disoriented when she scrambled out of the cave, blinking into the sunlight. Cautiously, she ventured away from the cave, flew to the top of the hill, and sat down on a large rock. Slowly the events of the previous night came back to her, and she quickly looked around to see whether she could detect the Goblins anywhere, but all appeared to be quiet.

"What a lucky escape I've had," she reflected about her close encounter with the Goblins. "I am ever so grateful Queen Orchidalia's protective charm is still so strong."

She looked around. Behind her lay the bog and in front of her more heathland. She suddenly felt lonelier than ever before. But then, she noticed larger hills and mountains in the distance. That must be the Highlands, King Teague's realm. She was nearly there. She allowed herself a large breakfast, not having eaten at all the day before, and set off again on her journey.

This time, she couldn't see anything following her, so she dared to rest in between, still feeling very exhausted from the adventures of the previous day. She managed to find a safe hiding place for the night, and after a lovely meal of Buttercup nectar, which she had been lucky enough to find, she spent an uneventful and restful night. Feeling much better the next day, Starflower set off early, eager to reach King Teague's kingdom by nightfall. Driven by the excitement of being so close to her destination, she made good progress and indeed reached the foot of the Highlands before dark.

I've made it! I'm nearly there! Tomorrow I can start looking for King Teague and ask him to make the elixir for Sundrop. I wonder how they are doing back home.

Thinking about her parents and Sundrop made her feel sad and alone, but she derived hope from potentially finding King Teague the next day. Slightly comforted, she went to sleep.

BACK AT HOME

How had Sundrop and the others been doing all this time? Their days had been rather uneventful compared to Starflower's adventures. Their preparations were nearly complete now, and they would soon set off to join the Stone Fairies. Without her wings, Sundrop couldn't do much to help and was both worried about Starflower and incredibly bored.

She had woven a mat from sturdy grasses, which would be fastened between two twigs to allow her parents to carry her on their journey to the Stone Fairies. It was large and sturdy enough to also hold several nectar-filled blossoms to make up for losing five pairs of hands to help carry them to the Stone Fairies. Each fairy would normally carry several of these blossoms to have enough food until November Eve and to give to the Stone Fairies. They also needed to keep some of it for when they would come out of hibernation again, to give them strength for their journey back home.

The days felt very long to Sundrop, although they

were getting significantly shorter. Just as Starflower had felt guilty and responsible for Sundrop losing her wings, Sundrop now felt guilty that she had allowed Starflower to go on such a dangerous journey for the sake of her wings.

I should've been more careful, she thought, *then none of this would've happened.*

She could hardly bear to look Meliantha in the eye whenever they met, which hadn't been too often lately. The two families were rather keeping to themselves these days.

Meliantha, who had always been close with her daughter, was equally riddled with guilt for having allowed Starflower to take on this burden. She couldn't bear seeing Sundrop, not because she blamed her for anything, but because she was a constant reminder that a similar fate could've befallen Starflower on her journey and she, her mother, wasn't there to help her.

"We should never have let her go," she often said to Trillium. He tried to comfort her, but couldn't really hide that he was just as worried. In two days, the Meadow Fairies would set off on their annual migration to the Stone Fairies, leaving only 16 days for Starflower to return in time. All of them were hoping Starflower was safe and had been able to find King Teague by now.

THE HIGHLANDS

The next day, Starflower rose in high spirits, eager to find King Teague. But after hours of searching, she had to admit that she had no idea where to look and how to find him or any of the Highland Fairies for that matter.

All the queen had told her was to look for them in old rabbit and fox burrows. But they all appeared to be empty or inhabited by the creature that had dug it. The Highlands were vast, and when the following day didn't bring any more success, Starflower was beginning to despair.

"What am I going to do? I've come all this way and now I can't find any Highland Fairy, let alone King Teague. If I don't find him soon, I'll never be able to make it back in time before November Eve. Oh, what shall I do?" she sobbed.

On her third day in the Highlands, she set off very early. A cold mist hung over the land. Starflower sniffed the air. Suddenly, a wisp of the strangest smell tickled her nose.

It was entirely unfamiliar to her, but pleasantly evocative of warmth, friendliness and a loving embrace. She followed the scent, which steadily grew stronger. Finally, she could see a soft glimmer of warm light through the slowly lifting mist. Getting closer, she saw that the light was coming from a rabbit burrow.

This must be it, she thought, feeling hopeful again. *This must be the dwelling of a Highland Fairy.*

She landed softly on the wet grass and slowly walked towards the burrow. At the entrance, she popped her head in and cautiously called, "Hello, is anybody here?"

She heard a noise like someone dropping something heavy, then a woman's voice said "Oh, my! Who could that be?" Then she heard footsteps coming towards her.

"Deary me, now this I would never have guessed. A Meadow Fairy at my door, this late in the season? Whatever brings you here, my dear? But do come in, you look like you're frozen to the bone."

In front of her stood a rosy-cheeked fairy, slightly taller and built much more sturdily than Starflower. She also wasn't translucent like Starflower. Her skin looked ruddy from perpetual exposure to the harsh elements in the Highlands. She wore a dress and cape woven from sheep's wool. Her wings were folded neatly on her back.

Before Starflower could say a thing, she was ushered to a seat in front of a cosy fire and was handed an acorn cupule filled with a hot liquid. Starflower had never had anything warm to drink in her life and was astonished by its scent. But more than that, Starflower had never seen the flames of a fire before! The warmth was lovely, but she was also scared it would burn her. She made sure to keep her wings well away from it.

"Don't worry, deary, the fire won't hurt you," said the Highland Fairy, reading the look on Starflower's face. "Take a sip of the dandelion tea, it will make you feel better."

Starflower took a sip and felt the warmth spread through her body. She looked around the dwelling. She sat on a mossy cushion. Nearby was a cosy bed made from moss and soft wool fluff. There was even a table and a couple of stools made from thicker and thinner branches. The delicious smell that had guided Starflower there came from a pan standing on a hot round stone next to the fire, the contents of which looked like a brown pebble.

"What is this?" asked Starflower, pointing to the pan. In her amazement, she did not realise that she hadn't even introduced herself yet.

"This is bread, dear. Would you like to try some? It's still warm," offered the kind fairy. "You must be from a long way away. By the way, my name is

Olinda."

"Oh, I am so sorry. I didn't mean to be rude. I'm just so amazed. I've never seen anything like this before. My name is Starflower, and I have indeed travelled a great distance. I must speak to King Teague urgently."

"King Teague? The king's cave is two day's journey further into the Highlands, deary."

Starflower's heart sank.

"I'll never get back in time!" she sobbed.

"Back in time for what?"

Starflower told Olinda everything about Sundrop, her adventure under the lakes with Alwen, and her encounter with the Goblins.

"Luckily, I found those little caves in a rock…" she was telling Olinda.

"Little caves in a rock?" gasped Olinda. "Oh my, you must indeed be well protected by Queen Orchidalia's charm. Evil spirits make caves like these and live together in colonies. I don't know if this was an abandoned colony or if you've been lucky not to run into them, but it is a miracle that you've not been hurt, or worse!"

"It will all have been for nothing if I can't make it

back in time."

"Now don't you worry, deary. You have a nice slice of bread with honey, while I go and find us a faster means of transport. Us Highland Fairies are rather slow on foot."

"You're coming with me?"

"But of course I will. I can't let you roam around the Highlands on your own."

"What do you mean by faster means of transport? Don't you fly?" asked Starflower curiously.

"No, we don't really use our wings much. Us Highland Fairies prefer to have our feet on the ground and a cosy home under it."

Olinda wrapped a woollen shawl around her shoulders and left Starflower with a slice of warm bread and golden honey. It was the most delicious food she had ever tasted.

A short while later Olinda returned.

"Let's go. Our ride is waiting outside. Here, take this cape. It will be much colder higher up in the Highlands, you'll need it."

She also packed the rest of the loaf and a jug of nectar in a basket. As they stepped outside the burrow, Starflower gasped. There, sitting in front of the burrow, was a hare! When it saw them approach, it lay down so they could scramble on.

"This is Reuben," said Olinda. "He's agreed to take

us to King Teague's cave. With his help, we'll be there before nightfall."

As soon as they'd nestled comfortably into the soft dip in his neck, Reuben hopped off. They were travelling at great speed. It was a bit bumpy and Starflower had to hold on tightly not to fall off during the occasional zigs and zags, but overall Starflower was very happy to give her wings a rest, and more importantly, that she was no longer travelling alone.

Reuben ran tirelessly. Around midday they stopped for something to eat. Olinda and Starflower feasted on bread and nectar, while Reuben nibbled on grass and the occasional dandelion. A chill wind blew, and it was getting much colder. Starflower was very grateful for the cape Olinda had given her. She was not used to these kinds of temperatures. After a short while, they were on their way again, climbing higher and higher into the Highlands. It was already getting dark when they finally arrived at King Teague's cave. Starflower was exhausted from the bumpy ride, but exhilarated that she had finally reached her destination.

I've made it. I'm finally here, she thought.

KING TEAGUE

Starflower and Olinda stood at the entrance to King Teague's cave, which was a triangular opening in the rock surface. A warm light emitted from inside, and cheerful music and singing reached their ears. Meadow Fairies like to hum gentle tunes and maybe play a flute made from hollow grass stalks. However, this was a very different sound. They could hear different drumming sounds and flutes that created a much richer sound than any grass stalk ever could. They heard the voices of many fairies singing, laughing and talking. Suddenly, Starflower got very nervous. How could she just show up unannounced and disturb this feast?

"There's nothing to worry about, dear," said Olinda, reading Starflower's expression. "Let's go in. I'm sure King Teague will make you most welcome."

Slowly they entered the cave. It soon widened into a large opening inside the rock. Starflower blinked for a moment in the bright light of several blazing fires. There were tables and stools like in Olinda's dwelling, but grander and larger. About fifty Highland Fairies were either talking merrily or twirling around to the music. King Teague was sitting on a large chair at the biggest table, laughing heartily. He had long, thick hair and a beard. His woollen cape was beautifully embroidered with heather and other Highland flowers. On his head were dried thistles, beautifully woven into a crown.

When Starflower was noticed, everyone fell silent and turned to see.

King Teague rose from his chair and walked over to Starflower.

"Now look at this, a Meadow Fairy in my cave. And such a young one, too. You come from the meadows in the South, don't you? What brings you to me, child?"

"I apologise for the intrusion, your Highness," said Starflower, who'd gone very shy. "Queen Orchidalia has sent me to you to ask for your help."

"It must be a grave matter indeed if Queen Orchidalia sends a young fairy such as yourself on this dangerous journey," said the king. "Come over to my table and tell me, what is the help you seek?"

Starflower and Olinda sat down at the table and Starflower told King Teague everything about Sundrop's wings and the elixir Queen Orchidalia required to perform the ritual.

King Teague frowned.

"You're quickly running out of time, dear Starflower. I will gladly help you, but the elixir has to brew for two days, and some of the ingredients will be hard to find this late in the season. But I'll do what I can. I'll begin first thing in the morning, there's nothing I can do now. So why don't you tell us about your adventures coming here?"

Starflower thanked the king for his help and told him and his guests, who by now had all gathered around the king's table, about everything she had experienced on the journey. She talked until late into the night, while they listened open-mouthed. Finally, everyone withdrew into a corner of the great hall or into smaller adjoining caves. Starflower was assigned a soft bed of moss and sheep's wool near one of the fires, similar to the one she'd seen at Olinda's, who was sleeping nearby. Despite being unbelievably tired and exhausted, Starflower couldn't sleep. Two more days before the elixir was ready! And that was provided they would find all the ingredients! How was she ever going to make it to the Stone Fairies in time?

As the fires slowly died down, Starflower saw that the cave ceiling was lit by glow-worms that looked like little stars in the dark sky. Starflower finally drifted off and dreamt of home.

The next morning, Starflower was awoken by the hustle and bustle in the cave. King Teague sat at a table, bending over a big book, calling a fairy's name every now and then, and sending them off on an errand. He looked up when Starflower approached.

"Good morning, Starflower," he smiled at her. "I hope you had a good rest? This must all be very strange to you indeed."

"Thank you very much for your kindness. Is there anything I can do to help?" She looked at the book that lay in front of the king.

"This is the Highland Fairy's Book of Healing," explained the king. "It has been handed down from king to king for generations. It contains all our knowledge of plants with healing powers and how to use them. It also contains a great many recipes for all kinds of maladies, not only for fairies, but animals, too."

The book was full of beautiful drawings of plants and flowers with signs she couldn't understand.

"This is the recipe for the elixir you require," said the king, pointing to a particular page. "I'm already sending out my fairies to find the ingredients. This one will be the most difficult to find," he said, showing Starflower the image of a bright red flower.

"Poppies are very rare this high up in the Highlands. By now they will have lost all their petals, too, so they will be difficult to spot. But Euan thinks he can remember the place where he saw some poppies in the summer, so he's gone there to look for one."

"Please, what can I do to help?" asked Starflower.

"You should rest and gather your strength. You have a long journey back, and not much time. The weather is getting more and more adverse, even down South. You'll need all the strengths you have. Now, have some breakfast. I believe Olinda is already waiting for you over there."

Starflower spent most of her time watching the elixir being prepared. Ingredients were added in a specific order and timing. Sometimes it had to be cooled, sometimes it had to be reheated. Once it had to be stirred continuously for two hours and then not be disturbed for the remainder of the day.

Every now and then Olinda managed to coax her away from her seat to take a walk. But it had gotten very cold, and Starflower preferred the warmth of the fire. So they talked a lot and exchanged stories of their folks. Starflower was interested but couldn't focus. She was anxious for the elixir to be finished, but for that, they still needed the final ingredient – the Poppy seeds. Euan still hadn't returned.

Around midday on the second day, he finally returned, waving a little pouch.

"They were really hard to find, but I got them," he laughed happily. Now the king could finish the elixir. Starflower was overjoyed.

"I'll set off first thing tomorrow morning," she exclaimed.

"Actually, you will leave tonight," responded the king.

Starflower looked at him in great surprise.

"Well, I thought, as you'd be cutting it a bit close with your journey home, I would find you a faster way to travel. At least for a part of your journey. But unfortunately, he only travels at night. Eat and rest now. The elixir will be ready at nightfall."

Starflower did as the king had recommended. By nightfall she was ready to start her journey back to the other Meadow Fairies, back to Sundrop, and back to her family.

"Thank you so much for bringing me here and for keeping me company. Here, I better give this back to you," she said and handed Olinda the woollen cape.

"Keep it. You will need it."

"How will you get back home?"

"Oh, don't worry about me, dear. I might actually stay a few days longer. Now, you make sure you take good care of yourself." Olinda gave Starflower a big motherly hug. Then they walked over to King Teague who was already waiting for her. He handed her the elixir that had been filled into a leather pouch that she could hang over her shoulder. Olinda had packed a little bit of bread and honey for her as well, which she had put into a small pocket in her cape.

"Follow me," said the king.

They walked outside. There was a fox sitting right outside of the cave. Starflower gave a shriek and jumped a few steps backwards. Foxes could be very dangerous to fairies.

"Don't worry, Starflower. This is Finnegan," said the king in an appeasing voice. "He will carry you all the way through the moors and heathland. I've heard about your encounter with the Goblins and your lucky escape from the evil spirits. Finnegan will get you to the lakes

in just three days, but as I said, he only travels at night, which means you will cross the moors in the dark. They are an unwelcoming place at the best of times, but most dangerous at night. You must stay invisible all night long, and find a safe place to sleep during the day. Do you understand?"

"Yes, I do. I will do exactly as you've told me. How can I ever thank you for your help and great kindness?" said Starflower.

"It was my pleasure. Please send my best wishes to your queen. I hope she'll come visit again in the spring.

You better be on your way now. Good luck!"

Starflower waved goodbye to everyone and fluttered up onto Finnegan's back. She nestled herself in between his shoulder blades and neck and turned herself invisible. Then they were off.

THE JOURNEY HOME

Finnegan ran like the wind. Travelling on a fox was much more comfortable than on a hare, but she still didn't dare to fall asleep in case she lost her grip on his fur in her sleep and fell off. She was too excited to finally be on her way back home anyway. Most of their journey in the first night was downhill back to lower ground. They both slept through the day and continued their journey at dusk. Tonight, they would pass over the moors. Starflower was a little scared, and buried her face in Finnegan's fur, holding on tightly. Finnegan navigated the moors with sure footing, and no-one and nothing disrupted their journey. Starflower still found the eerie noises and strange lights very disturbing, and buried her face even deeper into his fur. By dawn, they had left the moors well behind them and slept in an abandoned rabbit burrow. Her last night with Finnegan would take her through the heathland and back to the lakes. As soon as the sun came up, she saw them glisten in front of her. Finnegan stopped and Starflower left her comfortable seat on his back. She thanked

Finnegan for his help, who turned around to find a resting place for the day and then return to his own home.

Starflower flew to the edge of the lake. What had Alwen told her?

"Put your head in the water and call my name."

Starflower carefully took a few steps into the water. The water was icy-cold and it took her a while to submerge her head into it. Eventually she took a deep breath and dived in, calling out Alwen's name, but all that came out were some bubbles.

I hope she's heard me, Starflower thought. She was tired from the night's journey. Alwen wouldn't be able to rise to the surface before the sun had set again, so she had a good breakfast and found herself a safe place near the waterfront to sleep.

Starflower woke up in the afternoon and flew back and forth along the shoreline looking for Alwen's head popping up on the surface. It was getting darker and darker, but there was still no sign of her. Starflower was getting nervous that she might not have heard her or decided not to come after all. It was a very cold and clear night, allowing her to still see the surface of the water in the light of the moon. Suddenly, she heard her name being called in a coarse whisper from behind her. She turned around and saw Alwen's head bobbing up and down in the shallow waves of the lake.

"You came!" Starflower called, relieved.

"Of course I came!" responded Alwen. "I was getting worried something might have happened to you. I was expecting you days ago!"

"Oh, I know. First, I couldn't find King Teague, and when I had finally found him, it took two days to make the elixir, and…"

"Tell me everything on the journey. I'll take you to the other side of the lakes, but it will take two nights, as I'm not fast enough to cross all four big lakes in one night. I'll also have to renew the bubble, and that we can only do at night."

"Okay, I'm ready," said Starflower, and jumped into the dark cold water, but immediately felt the bubble forming around her, which also kept the coldness away.

Starflower had a lot to tell Alwen since they'd last seen each other, so the first night just flew by. Before the sun rose, Alwen surfaced, and Starflower flew to shore where they would meet again at nightfall for their second part of their journey together.

Starflower spend most of the day sleeping and awaited Alwen eagerly as soon as it got dark again. Their second night together was equally amiable, and when they reached the other side of the lakes, both girls were sad to say goodbye.

"I promise I'll come visit you again. If everything

goes well, I will bring Sundrop, too."

"I'll miss your company," responded Alwen sadly.

"Me too."

Then the sun rose over the horizon and they had to say their final farewells.

Starflower sat down by the side of the lake. The most dangerous parts of her journey lay behind her, but from now on she would be on her own again. She was tired from the night's journey, but could not afford to lose the entire day sleeping. She also hadn't seen much daylight in five whole days, and was keen to travel in the daytime again. She continued her journey for a few hours, but then she got too tired to continue any further.

For the next seven days, Starflower was entirely on her own. Heavy rainfall often forced her to stop and find shelter. Her cape was soaked with water and heavy around her shoulders, so she had to dispose of it, despite the cold. The days were much shorter, which didn't leave her many hours to continue her journey.

The meadows she passed were now abandoned and flattened by the rain. In her head, she was counting the days: "Four days until November Eve, three days until November Eve, two days…"

On the day before November Eve, things started to look familiar! It was flattened by the rain and wind, just like the others, but she definitely recognised certain places she and Sundrop had played together.

This was her meadow! Starflower was beside herself with joy. She had made it back! But the Stone Fairies were a good day's travelling away from her, and it was already getting darker. She wouldn't get there until the next day, even if she used up all of the remaining tonic. Would that still give Queen Orchidalia enough time to perform the ritual, or was she already too late? King Teague's elixir had taken two days to prepare, who knew how much time Queen Orchidalia needed to perform the ritual. Getting anxious, Starflower took a big sip of her strengthening tonic and pressed on.

NOVEMBER EVE

The last few weeks had been torture for Starflower's parents and Sundrop's family. Worry for Starflower's well-being paired with anxiousness for her return with the elixir made this usually very joyful time next to unbearable.

While the other Meadow Fairies mingled with the Stone Fairies, celebrating and exchanging stories, they had passed most of their time since their arrival in silence.

Today was November Eve, the day of the big celebration before they would go into hibernation, the day of the ritual that would regrow Sundrop's wings, the day Starflower would be reunited with her parents and best friend. But so far, there was no sign of Starflower – nor of Queen Orchidalia, for that matter. So many questions raced through their heads.

Was Starflower okay? Did she manage to get the elixir? Would she be here in time? Where was the queen?

Suddenly, they felt the warmth of renewed hope

pouring through their bodies and saw a brilliantly glimmering light coming toward them. The queen had arrived!

They weren't the only ones who'd noticed Queen Orchidalia's arrival. Everyone around them was in great excitement, inviting the queen to join the celebrations. She politely declined and eventually made her way to Sundrop and her family, who were now also joined by Starflower's parents.

"Oh, we're so grateful you're here," said Merrybell.

"Starflower hasn't returned yet," added Meliantha with an unmistakable tone of worry in her voice.

"I'm sure she'll be here any moment," said Queen Orchidalia soothingly. "I have everything with me for the ritual. Preparations took a bit longer than expected, hence my late arrival. All I need now is the elixir, but there's still time."

So they sat down together waiting for Starflower to arrive, while Queen Orchidalia explained the ritual.

"I'm afraid you will miss tonight's celebrations," she said to Sundrop. "As soon as Starflower arrives, we'll withdraw to your place of hibernation. In the first part of the ritual, we have to remove what is left of your wings. Don't worry," she added, seeing the look on Sundrop's face, "this won't hurt. Then in the second part, I'll apply King Teague's elixir and…"

"Mother?" said a shaking voice from behind them.

Their heads whipped around like an elastic band. Meliantha and Trillium jumped up and ran to their daughter, covering her in hugs and kisses.

"Oh, my dear child, you're back!" Meliantha cried, unable to let go of her beloved daughter, who looked wet and exhausted but extremely happy.

All of them were crying now with relief and happiness.

Starflower and Sundrop fell into each other's arms.

"I am so glad you're back. I was so worried. We should never have let you go," cried Sundrop.

"I've brought it back, Sundrop. The elixir. Now you can regrow your wings."

There was so much hugging and kissing and crying going on that they nearly forgot why Starflower had been away, and that there was still a ritual to perform.

"I'm sorry to interrupt this wonderful reunion," said the queen, "but we better start with the ritual. Sundrop, you and your parents should go to your cave now."

Then, turning to Starflower, she said, "You have done an incredibly brave thing for your friend. You should be proud of yourself. I most certainly am." Starflower handed her the elixir.

"When we wake up in the spring, I'll want to hear all about your journey. I'm sure you have many great stories to tell," added the queen.

"So do I," added Sundrop.

Merrybell and Vervain also gave Starflower a big hug, whispering, "Thank you!" into her ear, before the queen ushered them away to perform the ritual that would regrow Sundrop's wings.

Starflower and her parents spend a truly merry evening full of joy, laughter and many happy tears, as Starflower retold her adventurous journey. After the best meal of nectar Starflower had had in a long time, they retired hand in hand to their own place of hibernation. Starflower was wondering how the ritual was going, but she would have to wait until spring to find out. Meliantha wouldn't let go of Starflower's hand. Even as they settled down to hibernate, she held on tightly. Starflower loved it, and went to sleep with a smile on her face.

SPRING

Long months of cold, wind and darkness passed and slowly gave way to blue skies, warmer temperatures and the scent of daffodils and snowdrops.

Sundrop slowly started to move. A twitching finger here, a fluttering wing there.

My wings! I felt my wings! she thought. In a moment, she was wide awake. Around her lay her old shredded wings, and on her back was a pair of beautiful, perfect, fully-regrown ones!

Sundrop was overjoyed, squeaking with happiness that woke her parents.

Still a bit weak from the hibernation, but equally overcome with joy, they soon joined Sundrop, who was jumping around in excitement.

“I have to find Starflower!” she cried, racing off to find her.

Starflower was already awake, sipping on some nectar with her parents. She’d been weak and exhausted when she went into hibernation, and was in need of a good meal to give her strength. All of this was immediately forgotten, though, when she saw Sundrop racing towards her with her beautiful new wings. They fell into each other's arms, laughing and giggling and talking at the same time.

"It worked!" cried Starflower.

"All because of you! How can I ever thank you!" said Sundrop.

"I'm just so happy you've got your wings back."

"Now tell me everything about the journey," said Sundrop.

"Now, that I'd like to hear, too!" said a gentle voice.

Queen Orchidalia had also joined them. Together they sat down to eat, while Starflower told them about her first scary night in the reeds, Celandine and the other Meadow Fairies she'd met, Alwen the Asrai, Olinda, her travels on the back of a hare and a fox and her scary encounter while the Goblins and evil spirits.

When she had finished, the queen said "I have many great new stories to tell the other Meadow Fairies on my travels. You shall be an example of what a little Meadow Fairy can achieve when she puts her heart to it. But now," she said with a twinkle in her eye, "I think it's time for you to try out your new wings, don't you think, Sundrop?"

Sundrop and Starflower looked at each other, and giggling, fluttered off into the beautiful spring sunshine.

THE END

ABOUT THE AUTHOR

Ines Holmes is a UK-based German writer, and author of the 'Magical Tales from Fairyland' series. The idea for the series sparked from living in the beautiful countryside in the Southwest of England. "There are just so many hidden paths, enchanted forests and magical sunrises / sunsets here, that my imagination can run wild. It's truly magical."

Despite being a German native speaker, Holmes prefers to write in English and then translates the finished work into German. All illustrations are drawn by herself as well.

Printed in Great Britain
by Amazon

43730504R00056